THE HONEY BOAT

Polly Burroughs

THE HONEY BOAT

by Polly Burroughs

Illustrated by Garrett Price

4880 Lower Valley Road, Atglen, PA 19310 USA

"Having spent many years publishing children's books, I'm so pleased our original heartwarming tale of the Vinyard's salty, Yankee, Ellie and her garbage boat is being republished."

Arthur Thornhill
Former President, Little Brown & Co.

Text copyright © 2008 by Polly Burroughs
Illustrations copyright © 1968 by Garrett Price
Library of Congress Control Number: 2008925543

ISBN: 978-0-7643-3121-3
Printed in China

Schiffer Books are available at special discounts for bulk purchases for sales promotions or premiums. Special editions, including personalized covers, corporate imprints, and excerpts can be created in large quantities for special needs. For more information contact the publisher:

Published by Schiffer Publishing Ltd.
4880 Lower Valley Road
Atglen, PA 19310
Phone: (610) 593-1777; Fax: (610) 593-2002
E-mail: Info@schifferbooks.com

For the largest selection of fine reference books on this and related subjects, please visit our web site at
www.schifferbooks.com
We are always looking for people to write books on new and related subjects. If you have an idea for a book please contact us at the above address.

This book may be purchased from the publisher.
Include $5.00 for shipping.
Please try your bookstore first.
You may write for a free catalog.

In Europe, Schiffer books are distributed by
Bushwood Books
6 Marksbury Ave.
Kew Gardens
Surrey TW9 4JF England
Phone: 44 (0) 20 8392-8585;
Fax: 44 (0) 20 8392-9876
E-mail: info@bushwoodbooks.co.uk
Website: www.bushwoodbooks.co.uk
Free postage in the U.K., Europe;
air mail at cost.

I would like to thank George Price for his delightful illustrations.
The character of Ellie is based on a real person, but the rest of this story bears no resemblance to people or events in Edgartown.
The Author

To Rick
and
Horatio Hornblower

The harbor was quiet and still. Mist rose from the water in little wisps of smoke like steam from the spout of a teakettle, and the rising sun shone bright and clear.

A large figure loomed into view around the corner of the gray-shingled fish shed. Tattered bits of clothing streamed out behind as it stepped along the pier with a firm, sure stride, carrying a bundle of burlap bags. It was Ellie. Slowly, but majestically, she moved down the dock to her waiting skiff.

The little waves slapped softly against the sides of her rowboat when she pulled on the oars with short, firm strokes. Tying her dinghy to the moor-

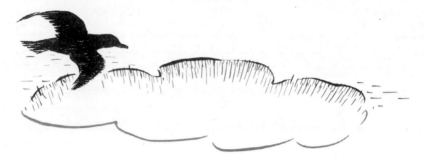

ing, she threw the bags into the cockpit of her cat-boat, *Dauntless*, and climbed aboard.

A sea gull squawked good-morning as he wheeled overhead and then glided down slowly, perching on the mast stub. He shrugged his wings and tucked them up neatly, waiting for breakfast. He was the same gull who had ridden with Ellie every summer for five years. She was sure, because the tip of one toe on his webbed foot was missing. Ellie always wondered whether it had been caught

in a clam shell, or perhaps some careless children had injured him. She would never know what had happened. But the gull never missed a day, rain or shine, and Ellie always gave him the best breakfast she could find.

She sat down in the cockpit and looked over her boat with pride—the kind of pride a skipper has who's devoted years of slow, careful work to keep his ship in tip-top condition. Every spring Ellie tuned the engine, scraped down the hull, puttied

the seams, and gave *Dauntless* a fresh coat of paint. Sturdily built and nearly as wide as she was long, *Dauntless*'s mast was only a stub, but years ago she had been used as a pleasure boat to take summer vacationers sailing. She was a work boat now, and her ancient engine pushed her along at a slow but steady five knots.

Ellie looked back at the row of white, whaling captains' houses, sedate and proud with their widow's walks, which lined the harbor front and sparkled in the morning sun. Turning east, she watched the little Chappaquiddick ferryboat, the *On Time*, crossing the harbor with its full load of two cars. The ferry was always on time because it had no time schedule.

Edgartown Harbor is formed by Chappaquiddick Island, a small island with several long, low sandspits and a few high hills covered with short, bushy pine trees, their growth stunted by the prevailing southwest winds. The island protects Edgartown Harbor from the Atlantic Ocean and provides a quiet place for boats to anchor.

She listened to the dull pa-thud-put, pa-thud-put, pa-thud-put of a fishing boat and watched

the pie-shaped wake bubbling astern as the boat slowly motored out past the lighthouse to the fishing grounds offshore.

The chiming of eight bells from the church tower was suddenly interrupted by a roar from the cannon on the yacht club pier which echoed across the harbor, while the launchman raised the American flag. That was the signal Ellie waited for, and she fired up her engine, cast off the mooring and started out.

Ellie had a very unusual job to do. No one else in all of Edgartown spent their mornings the way she did. Her job—and it was also her big interest in life—was to visit each boat in the harbor and

pick up the garbage and trash from the day before, put it in her burlap bags and cart it off to the dump. It was a messy, but very necessary job. The town paid Ellie a small, a very small sum of money every two weeks for her work. She didn't really mind the low wages so much—she liked to have things in the harbor clean and shipshape. In fact, she couldn't stand it if they weren't. Many a visiting skipper found this out the hard way.

She set about coiling her lines and piling up the burlap bags while *Dauntless* put-put-putted along. Overhead the gulls were screeching, arguing and scolding. They seemed to know Ellie was going to take it all—all that juicy garbage!

She pulled up alongside the port side of a lovely blue and white yawl. She put the engine out of gear, leaned over to grab the boat's rail, knocked on the deck with her free hand and called out, "Garbage Boat!"

The captain came up from below with three bags of trash.

"Don't just stand there. Take my line!" Ellie shouted impatiently to the man.

The captain put down his refuse and made the

line fast on a cleat. Smiling good-morning, he handed his garbage down to Ellie and she put it in the burlap bag, which was placed in a trash can for support.

Ellie's next stop was the *White Mist*, a large schooner where she knew Cindy would be waiting. The little girl was a real tomboy—barefoot and dressed in blue jeans and a boy's shirt. Her long blond hair and bangs were the only girlish thing about her. The Palmer family lived aboard *White Mist* all summer, and Ellie took Cindy on the garbage route every day unless the weather was particularly severe. The little girl loved it and was overjoyed when Ellie taught her how to handle the lines, steer *Dauntless*, and pile up the garbage bags neatly. Ellie always paid her twenty cents at the end of the week for her help.

Cindy caught the line Ellie tossed, and took a halfhitch on the cleat, just as she had been taught. Then she helped pass the bags of garbage down to Ellie and climbed aboard.

"There's a heap of boats in today," Ellie explained, "and we'll be on our beam-ends if we don't load her careful-like."

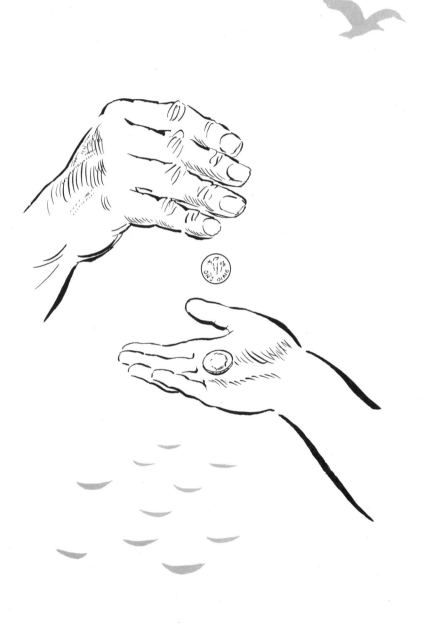

"Can I skipper?" Cindy asked.

"'Course you can, Cindy. It'll be calm for a spell—'spect it'll blow up nor'east later. Keep her steady as she goes. That'a girl."

A bugeye, a large sloop and a ketch all had their garbage ready when they motored up to the side Ellie called the back door. The skipper of one boat, who didn't want to be awakened so early in the morning, had carefully tied up his trash the night before and put it out in his dinghy.

This boat always had the best garbage in the harbor—clean and expensive. Ellie sifted it out until she found some muffins and lettuce leaves. She took the tiller while Cindy fed the gull, which was her favorite job aboard *Dauntless*.

The bird gobbled it down quickly and squawked for more.

"Hush up! You'll bust a boiler with all that squawkin'! That gull's a glutton!" Ellie shouted, impatiently.

"Oh, please," Cindy begged, "he looks sad. Just give him one more piece of lettuce."

"Well—O.K.—just one more piece. If he don't

quiet down now I'll skin him for shark bait."

Cindy was delighted to see the gull preen himself and settle down. She wasn't sure whether or not Ellie was serious.

They were approaching a large yacht when Ellie spotted several bags of garbage floating down through the harbor. She told Cindy to speed up the engine and they quickly caught up with the debris, which Ellie scooped up. She was furious! She had always wondered about this

fancy yacht. Too many gulls hanging around the stern! She took the tiller from Cindy, spun the *Dauntless* around and headed over.

"Garbage Boat!" she called out.

"We don't have any," the skipper replied, coming up from below.

"You mean you don't eat? No trash at all?" Ellie asked.

"No, no. Nothing today," the skipper replied, and took refuge down below.

"He's a tonguey one, he is. City folk, you can be sure," Ellie muttered to Cindy. And with that she took the three bags of garbage and threw them on deck.

The skipper heard the splattering thud as the bags landed and burst open, the soaking mess sliding across his clean decks. He rushed topsides.

"What do you think you're doing?" he screamed at Ellie, shaking his fist.

"Go chase yourself! What do you think YOU'RE doin'? Next time you don't have any trash I'll be tellin' the harbor master. Some folks'll say anything but their prayers. Go dump your own dirty garbage!" Ellie called back at him as *Dauntless* whirled about and headed for a large sloop.

"What're you so quiet for today? Sumpin' wrong?" Ellie asked Cindy.

"Oh, it's nothin'," Cindy replied, hanging her head.

"Well, it IS sumpin'! Come on now—out with it," Ellie said in a firm voice. "You'll bust a boiler yourself."

"It's just that my Mother won't let me go

fishin' alone! Says I'm too small. She wants me to play dolls with some friends. I HATE dolls!" Cindy blurted out, stamping her foot.

"Calm down. Hold on. Things like this can work out. Leastwise you can skipper a boat. And you're some smart—know that? You'll be able to go fishin' alone in no time. Can't do everythin' at once. Besides, it's good to play with someone your own age once in a while."

"I guess so," said Cindy.

"Look out where you step. Don't slip on the sour cream," Ellie cautioned as Cindy moved back to take the tiller. "Enough to ruin a good garbage bag. Makes you wonder about some folks—can't ever put a top back."

Ellie had given Cindy the tiller again and *Dauntless* eased up beside the next boat.

"Garbage Boat!" Ellie called out.

"How much does it cost?" asked the captain.

"If I want your money I'll say so. And it don't come in smelly paper bags. Are you goin' to hand her over or stand there? I got a heap of work to do."

"Money! Humph! More fancy trimmin' on that boat than a Sunday bonnet and he don't know nothin' 'bout keepin' a harbor clean. That figgers," Ellie grumbled, while the skipper went below and returned with several bags. He seemed embarrassed and didn't say a word.

It was noon before they finished. They had visited every boat in the harbor and *Dauntless* was loaded to the gunwales.

"Well, Cindy, we're all finished for today," Ellie said as they pulled up to *White Mist* and Cindy scrambled aboard.

"Hey, skipper, ain't you forgot sumpin'?" Ellie called. "Not havin' you aboard is like chowder without clams. Here's your twenty cents."

"Gee, thanks, Ellie. See you tomorrow." Cindy waved from the schooner's deck.

"Shucks, ain't nuthin'," Ellie called back, spinning *Dauntless* around.

Ellie was put-put-putting along slowly toward the town pier when suddenly, out of nowhere, three boys zoomed by in an outboard, just missing *Dauntless* by inches!

"Pew! Pew! Pew! Look at the fat old lady in

the funny honey boat! Pew! Pew! Do you stink!"
they yelled at Ellie.

"Get outa here—keep away!" she cried, jumping up just as the wake hit the boat and threw Ellie across the cockpit in a heap on the floor. She scrambled up to grab the tiller.

"Drive it or milk it!" the boys shouted and swung in again, and then raced up harbor. Another large wave struck *Dauntless* and Ellie lunged forward at the same time, struggling to keep the garbage bags from rolling off the foredeck. The side of her foot caught on the floorboard and her ankle buckled under, sending a sharp pain up through her leg. The gull was jolted off the mast stub. Screeching and flapping, he finally regained his balance and sat down.

"You just wait till the harbor master hears about this! I'll get ya yet!" she shouted after the boys.

The burning pain in her ankle became worse and her whole foot began to throb so much she had to sit down. Slowly she headed for the town dock again.

"What's the matter with you?" one of the fishermen standing alongside the fish shed called, as Ellie pulled *Dauntless* alongside the pier.

"Shucks, ain't nothin'," Ellie replied. "Could be a dum sight worse. Can't have the peace of mind of a dog with them kids out there. Say, gimme a hand, will ya?"

The fisherman helped Ellie load her bags of trash into the back of the jeep. She motored back to the mooring and tied *Dauntless* up for the night. The pain made it very difficult for her to get into her skiff and row back to the pier. She hobbled into her jeep and drove off to the town dump. There was a huge flock of whining, screeching gulls waiting for her, and Ellie usually had some harsh words for them, but tonight her swollen ankle hurt so much she hardly noticed they were there. After she had finished, she went home and fell into bed.

Cindy waited all the next morning for Ellie, but she never came. Day after day the little girl got up bright and early to look for her friend. It was always the same. The empty boat lay still, tied to its mooring, and the gull sat patiently on the mast stub just as though he expected Ellie to ar-

rive any minute. Cindy couldn't imagine what had happened to her friend.

And no one came to collect the garbage from the boats. The boatmen became very sloppy and lazy. First one threw his trash overboard, then another and another. Each felt that if the others were doing it, then he too could throw his garbage in the harbor.

Old newspapers, beer cans, milk cartons, orange and grapefruit peels, oil cans and soda bottles floated in messy patches of debris in the harbor and littered the once clean, white beaches.

Still there was no Ellie. Cindy finally couldn't stand it any longer and asked her mother if she could go and find out what had happened to her friend.

She took the launch in to the pier, and the launchman pointed out Ellie's house up over the hill.

Cindy ran up the road as fast as she could to the little, gray, ramshackle house and, very softly, knocked on the door.

"Come in," a voice called, and Cindy slowly opened the door. She was shocked! There, in a

simple iron bed, lay Ellie. She had one table, a little coal stove, and two wooden chairs. The room was cluttered with dirty dishes, glasses and old magazines.

"What's the matter?" Cindy asked.

"Oh, nuthin'. Nuthin' at all," Ellie replied.

"But you haven't been out to *Dauntless* in more than a week! And you're in bed. There is something wrong!" Cindy insisted.

"Been just a bit tuckered, but shucks, ain't nothin' now, Cindy. Sprained my ankle—that's all."

"You shouldn't be here alone, Ellie. Please come back to our boat—there's plenty of room."

"Now don't go frettin'. The doctor come and he says I'll be up in no time. Jest that I need to rest a bit—that's all. Now git on back to the schooner—hurry up—scat! I'll be aboard *Dauntless* in no time."

Cindy fought to hold back the tears as she walked slowly down the road to the launch. When she got to the schooner, her mother assured her Ellie would be all right.

That evening Cindy and her parents had dinner at the Seaside Inn instead of on their boat. While they were having dessert, a man two tables away suddenly started to groan. His face was white and after a moment he put his head down on the table. His dinner companions helped him up, and the restaurant owner quickly called the town ambulance, which came and took him to the hospital.

This was the first Cindy and her family saw of the mysterious sickness that was suddenly striking the people of Edgartown. The next day Cindy's father showed them an item in the *Vineyard Gazette*. The man at the Inn was only one of a number of people who had suddenly been taken ill and were flat on their backs at home or lying in the town hospital. The town's two doctors rushed about answering emergency calls and they became increasingly worried and exhausted as the number of sick people grew. And, worst of all, they had no idea what was making everyone sick.

The health officer and the two doctors were very puzzled. It didn't seem to be one of the contagious diseases. And it wasn't like anything they were used to. The symptoms were fever, headache, diarrhea and vomiting. Some people were sicker than others, some had only one or two of the symptoms. The doctors decided to ask each patient a number of questions and then study the answers. Maybe this way they could get some clue.

But there was a big problem. The hotel guests came and went, the boats were in and out of the harbor and it was only those in their own homes, or in the hospital, who could give them the detailed information they needed.

The health officer thought it might be something they were eating—in fact he was almost sure the meat had gone bad. He took samples from all the grocery stores, hotels and restaurants in town and went back to his laboratory to test them. After studying for several days he complained to the doctors and the Mayor, "There's nothing wrong here at all. And I was so certain. We must keep searching."

"If it's not a contagious disease, and they aren't eating bad meat, what could it be?" asked the Mayor, wrinkling his brow and shaking his head.

"We'll have to keep searching," replied the health officer. "That's all we can do."

Cindy hadn't become sick herself, but she had heard all the talk. Although Ellie had told her not to come back, the little girl felt she just had to go and see how her friend was getting along. So she hurried back to the little house over the hill.

Cindy told Ellie how everyone in town seemed to be getting sick and no one knew what caused the Edgartown epidemic.

"'Spect them doctors will find out what'sa matter, Cindy. Leastwise, that's their job," Ellie replied.

"Can you come back soon?" Cindy asked. "The harbor's awful dirty now without you collectin' the trash."

"You mean to say there ain't anybody collectin' the garbage? And they're throwin' it all in the harbor? Thunderation! Why, I'll bet even the fish wish they'd gone offshore in that mess. Cindy!"

Suddenly Ellie sat up, her eyes wide. "Cindy! Them folks might'a been eatin' bad fish. Now you run on back and tell your Pa to tell them experts to check the fish."

Cindy was very excited about having such important news and hurried back to the schooner. The sun was setting behind the lavender and pink clouds which streaked the horizon and the lighthouse was flickering like a firefly in the dusk when Mr. and Mrs. Palmer came back to the boat from doing errands. When they heard Cindy's news they immediately got in touch with the health officer.

Edgartown is on an island, out at sea, and for this reason it had never occurred to anyone that the beautiful, clean-looking water might be dirty. But just to be sure, the health officer took samples of fish from the local market and from the fishermen themselves to test in his laboratory.

He put bits of fish flesh in a blender and beat it up very fine. Then he put some of this mixture in a petri dish, which is a shallow, round glass dish with a cover, and he sealed it up tight. Then he waited.

After several days, the health officer went back to look at the smears of fish flesh under his microscope. He had learned to identify the many different-shaped cells the way people identify flowers. Some were octagonal, some round or fluted, some looked like little worms, and some were almost diamond shaped. If the fish were tainted, he would see cells of a certain definite shape.

He looked for a long time. He studied each sample carefully.

"There's nothing wrong with the fish at all," he assured the town authorities. "That's not our problem."

"Did you test the clams, too?" asked one of the doctors.

"Not much sense in that. If the fish are fine, certainly the clams will be too," replied the health officer. "But I guess we should try everything. Ten more were reported ill today. I'll make a test anyway."

He took some clams and seawater and ground them up fine in a blender, just as he had done with the fish. Then he put some samples in a petri dish and set them aside for a few days.

The doctors continued their search for more clues. Each day new cases of illness were reported and there seemed to be no stopping this mysterious epidemic. The Mayor, the health officer and the doctors had a meeting and decided they must call in extra help from one of the medical centers to work with them. While they were discussing this, the health officer was bent over his microscope studying the clam culture.

"Mmmm—this is strange. Come look at those cells clustered together—little round disks. Look at those cell walls, and the yellowish color. This isn't normal. We must do more tests."

The doctors gathered around. The health officer put different stains and dyes in the clam mixture and tried different temperatures to see what would happen. The men worked day and night studying the clams.

Finally, after a few days, the health officer had the answer. "Gentlemen, these clams are contaminated. It is dysentery which has made everyone who's been eating clams taken from the harbor sick. It seems impossible . . . but the harbor must be polluted. Let's go see for ourselves."

No one had thought before to take a careful look at the harbor. They were horrified. The water was littered with floating garbage!

"Why is it so dirty?" asked the Mayor.

"I've never seen such a dreadful mess!" exclaimed the health officer. "What happened? Where's Ellie?"

"She's in bed with a sprained ankle," replied a fisherman standing by. "Seems some boys went zooming by her in an outboard and she lost her footing."

"Oh yes, I remember," said one of the doctors. "I strapped up her ankle. But I never thought to ask her about the garbage collection. How stupid of me!"

"I'll go see her immediately," replied the Mayor. He started off.

Word about the harbor spread quickly and the townspeople swarmed down to the harbor front to see for themselves. Seizing the opportunity, the doctors put them right to work, cleaning up. Fishing boats, work boats, pleasure boats, visiting yachtsmen in their dinghys and boys in rowboats all gathered to help pick up the debris. Scallopers used their drags to pull garbage off the bottom and people on the beaches picked up papers, cans and bottles. They piled it all on the town dock, where men were waiting in jeeps and trucks to

haul it off to the dump to be burned. The harbor master went about arresting everyone who had thrown trash in the harbor.

The police cruised around town announcing on a loudspeaker that no one was to eat any clams or shellfish until further notice. Signs were posted everywhere and restaurants were prohibited from serving shellfish. The town officials were glad they had caught it before things got any worse. If it had gone on much longer, the fish might have been affected.

The Mayor found Ellie in her shack, hobbling around the stove. He told her about the bad clams and how dirty the harbor had become.

"I better get down there," Ellie exclaimed. "Thunderation! People might'a kept things clean on their own!"

"You stay right here, Ellie. You're valuable property—this town is just beginning to realize how valuable! Rest up until your ankle is better."

"No—no! Shucks, my ankle ain't so bad now. I got to see for myself."

Ellie insisted, and she limped down to the harbor front with the Mayor to see the massive cleanup. She hobbled out on the town pier and began shouting orders to the men.

"Don't leave a paper, bottle or bone!" she yelled at the men. "Look behind ya!" she shouted at one fisherman.

"Ah, come on Ellie. Don't be so goldarn fussy!" the man yelled back at her.

"Git it all. You heard me! Ain't no use cleaning if you can't put it to right," Ellie called back.

The fisherman muttered to his helper: "She'd be a good one to have on board in a calm. She never shuts up. You git her talkin' abaft the mains'l and you'd have a twenty knot breeze in no time."

But Ellie heard him and she was in no mood for such remarks.

"Garbage is my business and garbage it'll be. The only thing you ever stuck to was the day you set on the bench you'd just painted."

It took almost a week of good hard work before the harbor was finally clean. And it might take many weeks before the water purified itself and was no longer polluted. Every day the authorities went down to the harbor front and took fresh

samples of water and shellfish to be tested in the laboratory.

The fishermen, who had often made fun of Ellie and her honey boat, began to see how very important her job had been. And the visiting yachtsmen realized that a small bit of garbage tossed overboard could be very serious. No one was likely to make fun of Ellie again.

The townspeople and the town officials decided they must somehow show their gratitude to Ellie for what she had been doing all this time. Everyone had been taking Ellie's work for granted for too long. So they declared the following Saturday "Ellie Day."

A large group gathered down on the town dock for the celebration. The man who owned the local shipyard spoke up and said he would refinish and paint Ellie's boat for nothing. Then the Mayor made a very fine speech, praising Ellie for her work. Afterward he read a letter of thanks from the town officials, stating that her salary would be doubled.

The audience cheered when Ellie limped up to the speaker's stand. She stood in front of the microphone to speak, but it bothered her. She brusquely pushed it aside, and in her best garbage boat voice called out, "Shucks, it ain't nothin'. Things kind of average up in this world. Come on, Cindy—we got some work to do and you can skipper today."

Everyone clapped and cheered again as Ellie hobbled down to the dock with the little girl trailing behind her.

"Good to be back on the job," Ellie said as she fired up *Dauntless*'s engine. "And there won't be a paper, bottle or bone left in the harbor when we get finished, now will there?"